A PUG SAVES CHRISTMAS

A Heartwarming, Cozy and Festive Story for Dog Lovers

By Jenn Somerville

COPYRIGHT

JOIN MY MAILING LIST

Subscribe to my mailing list so that you never miss any of my new releases, promotions or freebies.

Click on https://fantastic-builder-2533.ck.page/b554c54593

PUG IN PURGATORY

The lights went out and within a few seconds, the main door to the dog shelter slammed shut. A howl could be heard, and then a few other dogs started barking. In the far corner of the shelter, in a little kennel on his own, was a little Pug called Winston. He stopped walking around his kennel and sat back down on his blanket.

His kennel resembled something more akin to a prison cell. With a place for his toilet, a food and water dispenser, and a blanket for his bed, there was nothing else to occupy his mind. Each kennel had bars up to prevent the dogs escaping, and it was designed so that the dogs could only see the kennel opposite theirs. However, the kennel opposite Winston's was currently empty. The floor of the kennel was made of stone and was very cold. Even the hardiest of dogs found the stone floor chilling. Poor Winston kept on raising his pads off the ground to prevent them getting too cold.

He looked sorrowfully down at the floor. His last best friend had just been taken away today. Maisie, the Puggle, had resided at the shelter for only a few days but they had gotten along well, sharing a kennel together. Maisie had loved to play and had been so fun-loving. They had loved their time together, however fleeting it had been. For it hadn't been very long at all before a nice person had come along and snapped up Maisie, leaving Winston behind again. *Why don't they ever pick me?* thought Winston. He wondered if he would ever see Maisie again. He hoped so. She had made his life worth living for those few blessed days. But now he was all alone and none of the visitors to the shelter appeared to want him. Yes, they cooed at him and they held him gently and stroked him, but not one of them would take him home with them.

What was not to like about Winston? Yes, he was smaller than a normal sized Pug. But he was only 4 years old, and he had the most beautiful creamy brown coat. His eyes looked sad, but then all other Pugs' eyes did too. He had a wonderful calm temperament and he loved being with people and with other Pugs. He was very laid back and he enjoyed playing with toys. Winston thought he was the best dog an owner could ever have. *So why didn't they pick him? Why was he still here after three months?* He couldn't understand it.

The barking continued in the pitch black. The owner of the shelter had gone for the night, and the dogs would be left alone till the next morning. They had 14 hours of darkness to endure before the owner came back the next day and opened up the shelter again.

Winston looked up. He could hear something from outside. The sound of human voices drifted through, ever so faintly. The barking suddenly stopped, as if all the dogs were listening intently to what was going on outside. Winston strained to hear. His little ears could just about make out a few people singing. They sounded happy and joyous. If Winston had been able to see through walls, he would have seen a crowd gathered outside the dog shelter, in the centre of town, singing and playing the Christmas song, 'Joy to the World'. Their voices sounded uplifting as they continued to sing, and Winston could now clearly make out the music. It must be Christmas. That was a song he had heard before. It was sung at Christmas time.

The choir men and women sang their hearts out as passers by stopped to listen and take in the beautiful music and singing. Snow fell silently and gently around them as the choir continued singing. It was a cold December winter's evening, and the people of the town were Christmas shopping and sampling food and drink in the nearby Christmas market. Christmas lights were strewn across the town, from building to building, and the town's main Christmas tree stood majestically tall in front of the town hall, with its lights shining bright for all to see. People busied themselves, walking in and out of the local shops and eateries. Some carried bags of shopping; others walked around just taking in the atmosphere, the smells and the sounds. They were all dressed for the occasion; overcoats, warm winter fleeces, boots, gloves, and hats. Each bar and restaurant that people walked past looked so inviting, with a roaring fire in the fireplace, a Christmas tree by the window, and cosy armchairs to sit down in and relax. As the snow fell outside, customers sat as close as they could to the fire and reminisced about Christmases past and present.

Inside the dog shelter, the dogs continued to remain silent as they listened to the Christmas choir's rendition of 'Silent Night'. Winston recognised it. He loved Christmas. Previously, he had been owned by the Wilson family. They had always made a fuss over him, and they had been very loving. Every Christmas, Winston had been spoiled and he had wanted for nothing. He had usually ended up eating too many treats and felt a bit sick, as his hunger knew no bounds. He would keep on eating, given half a chance. Each Christmas had been a joyous occasion, and the family had celebrated it together.

But something had changed a few months ago. The father of the household had moved out, and the mother and her two children had seemed very sad. The father never returned, and Winston noticed that food was more scarce and that when he was ill, they didn't take him to the vets like they used to. Eventually, the mother and two children had moved out of the house. On removal day, the children were at school and it was just the mother and Winston together in the house. She had held Winston in her arms and wept inconsolably. Tears had dropped onto Winston as he lay in her arms, and she told him that she was sorry. When the removal men had come to take all of the furniture away, the mother had driven Winston to the dog shelter. After a few minutes, and again inconsolable with tears, she had left Winston behind. He hadn't seen her or the children since, and he missed them terribly. For the first month, Winston had eagerly awaited their return. Every time there had been a visitor at the shelter, Winston had pricked up his ears to listen to their voices and had used his amazing sense of smell to determine if the visitors were members of his old family. When he had eventually seen the visitors face to face, he had realised that his suspicions were correct, and the family had not come back to bring him home.

With every day that passed, Winston's hopes faded more and more. He knew that he had been abandoned, and he wondered why. He had shown them love and affection, He had been a well-behaved dog. He was good natured, friendly, and caring. He just didn't understand what had happened, and how he had ended up in this prison cell. Christmas this year was gonna be very different to previous years. The owner of the shelter, Bob Fletcher, might throw them a few scraps of turkey. On the other hand, he might shut the shelter for a couple of days and leave them in the dark for even longer than usual.

As the sound of the choir became more distant, Winston lay back down on his blanket. He was not looking forward to Christmas this year.

COFFEE AND CAKES

Alison sat down at a nice table, right by the fireplace. The fire was burning gently, and the warmth from it began to thaw Alison's face. She took off her winter coat, gloves and hat and lay them down on the seat next to her. She looked over at the counter. Her friend Louise was standing at the cash register. Beneath her was a glass cabinet with an array of beautiful baked goods. You name it, they had it. Scones, cakes, bread, sandwiches, quiche, pies. Louise was chatting to the guy at the register, asking him questions about something.

Alison looked around the hostelry. It was a beautifully old building that had been converted from an old barn into a posh eatery, with comfy armchairs, mahogany coffee tables, and warm and cosy furnishings. The place was adorned with a plentiful array of Christmas decorations and there were a couple of small Christmas trees with lights shining bright. The tables were full of people enjoying a morning cup of coffee and a piece of cake or a scone. They all seemed very happy; after all, it was only a few more days till Christmas.

This place was Alison's favourite, yet she usually had very little opportunity to visit it. Being a single mother and self-published author, she had very little time to herself. She hadn't seen her friend Louise for over a month. They had decided to meet before Christmas, and Alison had suggested they meet here. It was a nice place, in the centre of town, and she was desperate to try the Death by Chocolate Cake again! That cake was literally to die for.

Louise walked over to the table and said, 'They are going to bring our order over....Sorry about that, but I just had to look at all of those gorgeous cakes. And when I did, it made it even harder to decide what to have'.

Alison laughed and said, 'That's why I don't look. Anyway, my order is always the same here. I would never forgive myself if I didn't get the chocolate cake'.

Louise smiled. 'It's been a while since we caught up. How is everything? And how is Becky?'

'Everything is as well as it could be. Becky is doing well, you know. It's a bit lonely for her now that she has to home school, but I try my best to keep her chin up. She is such a lovely, caring girl. And very determined when she puts her mind to something. I am very lucky to have her'.

'Ah Alison, that's lovely. She is a beautiful girl - inside and out. I have always thought that', replied Louise. She then looked over to the baristas who were making the coffees. As she did, Alison noticed that Louise was beginning to show her age. Like Alison, she was 45 and the lines under her eyes were beginning to show. And she was a little overweight. But she still had a lot going for her. She hadn't lost her good looks. Her beautiful shoulder length auburn hair hadn't changed a bit; it complemented her face, and she still looked stunning. Alison and her had been good friends for a long time, ever since their children had joined the same nursery. And though they saw a lot less of each other, they were still great friends and could call on each other in times of need.

'How are your two, Louise?'

Louise turned to look back at Alison. 'You know, they are doing well but Felicity is 13 so she is becoming a bit of a handful, to be honest. The terrible teens!'

Just then, the barista came over with their food and drink. A young lad of about 20 years old, tall and slim with short black hair, brought over Alison's cafe latte and death by chocolate cake, along with Louise's hot chocolate and cream horn. As he put them down, both Alison and Louise licked their lips in anticipation.

'Have you decided what to get Becky for Christmas?' asked Louise.

'Well, I have decided, yes. But it's a bit of a touchy subject! Becky wants a dog for Christmas! And I always said that I wouldn't get her a dog for Christmas. I've always drilled it into her that a dog is not just for Christmas. But in the circumstances, I think I am going to get her one. But I've only just realised that new puppies are just so darn expensive', said Alison.

'You're telling me. I paid $3000 dollars for our little Beagle', said Louise. 'Maybe you could look in the dog shelter for an unwanted dog'.

Alison took a sip of latte and held the cup in both her hands, warming them up from the cold outside. 'I think I will have to go there. I can't afford to go anywhere else. Only problem is - I think Becky needs a nice natured dog. I don't think she could cope with a badly behaved one. I have seen one dog on the shelter's website and I have been speaking to the dog shelter manager for a few weeks now'.

'What kind of dog?'

'He's a four year old Pug, and he's called Winston. He looks adorable'. Alison pressed on her phone screen and brought up a picture of Winston from the website.

'Oh Alison, he's adorable. Such a sad looking face, but he looks really cute. But dare I ask - how come there is a pug in the dog shelter? They are normally snapped up'.

Alison couldn't answer straight away, as she had just eaten a chunk of chocolate cake and was savouring the mouthful. She closed her eyes for a second; it was 'that' good. Louise chuckled at her and then looked around the room. Everyone seemed happy, chatting away. Some were wearing Christmas jumpers. Others were wearing traditional Christmas colours of red, brown and green. She then looked at the fireplace next to them, and felt the warmth of the fire against the side of her body. The room and the atmosphere all felt very Christmassy.

Having savoured her mouthful of cake, Alison said, 'Yes, the poor little guy has had cancer. Cancer of the lymph nodes. Poor thing'.

Louise felt so sorry for the little guy. Her face dropped and her eyes lowered. 'That's awful, Alison. Really awful.....is he terminal?'

'No, he's not terminal. He's been taking chemotherapy tablets and he is currently in remission. But I guess people don't want to take him in case he costs them too much...or if he gets ill again, they might only get a few months with him'.

'I am still surprised no-one has taken him in. I thought that sad face would melt anyone's heart'.

'I think it must be the cancer. I guess they are put off. The cost, inconvenience, and he may only live a short while longer. I have one worry - I would hate it if Becky grew really attached to him over say a month or two, and then we had to say goodbye to him....It would break my heart'.

'I think it's a chance worth taking', said Louise. 'Someone needs to give him a loving home. And you and Becky will certainly do that. Have you decided to take him?'

Alison looked at the fire, contemplating what she should do for the best. The flames flickered brightly and the warmth from the fire radiated over her. 'I've made enquiries, and I am supposed to go see him tomorrow morning'.

'If I were you, I would definitely take him. Becky will adore him'.

'Yeah, the more I think about it, the more I think it's the right thing to do. I think my heart will melt when I see him tomorrow. He looks so sad and helpless. I bet he is really depressed in there. I don't think they treat the dogs very well. It's a disgrace, really', said Alison.

'Rescue him. You won't regret it', said Louise.

Just then, the front door opened and in walked a lady dressed in an overcoat, winter hat, gloves, waterproof trousers and boots. With her was a little pug. It had a pink bow on its leash and it looked very happy. The lady said, 'Where shall we sit, Maisie?' She looked around for a seat and then looked at the specials menu board above the counter and the coffee machines.

Louise and Alison both looked at her and the pug.

'You see, Alison. It's a sign. Just as you were debating whether to take Winston, in walks a pug. I think you should take him. Poor little guy needs a home'.

'Yeah', replied Alison. 'I think I should snap him up before someone else does'. She then jabbed her fork into another large chunk of chocolate cake, looked at it for a moment, and then slowly put it in her mouth. Louise looked on as Alison found herself in chocolate heaven.

ALISON'S VISIT

The main entrance door was opened, and in walked the owner of the dog shelter, Bob Fletcher. He was in his fifties, balding, overweight and unkempt. He wore the same baggy uniform that he always did. And this job was not his calling. He didn't really care about the dogs. Granted, he didn't want to see them suffer too much, but above all else, making money was his most important consideration. Profits came first, and animal welfare was second.

As he opened the door that morning, he lumbered his way in and sighed when he heard the barks and the whimpers from all the dogs. The light from outside came blasting into the main room and all the dogs had to readjust their eyes to the light. The main corridor in the shelter was long and narrow. On either side were kennels with individual dogs, or sometimes with two dogs. The cleanliness in the shelter left a lot to be desired. Bob would only clean the kennels when he had to, and he did not show the dogs any affection or love.

'Ah, shut up!' he shouted, clearly frustrated with all the noise from the dogs. Some stopped barking, but others continued. Bob went into the food storage area, and started organising which dogs needed their daily medication.

Winston remained prone on his dog blanket. He had heard all of the commotion, but just lay there in abject silence. He was very unhappy and wished that he could return to his old family, but he knew that it was unlikely to happen. He heard the other dogs whimpering and barking and it made him feel sad for himself and for them. He wished he could see their faces, but all of the dogs were placed in separate kennels and they weren't able to see each other.

Bob walked down the corridor and when he found a dog that needed medication, he dispensed it and then moved on. As he continued on his way, Winston could hear him shout, 'Stop barking, you stupid mutt!' and he also heard Bob hit one of the dogs hard. The thwacking noise sent reverberations around the shelter, and Winston looked down at the ground when he heard it. His mood remained morose and melancholic.

When Bob arrived at Winston's caged door, Winston quickly got up off his blanket and opened his eyes wide to try to readjust to the daylight that was flooding in from outside. He yawned and looked up at Bob's face, which was glaring down at him.

'Still can't get rid of you! No one wants you, do they?' shouted Bob. 'Never had an unwanted Pug before. You are my first. You know what your problem is, Winston? If you fall ill again, then you will need more chemotherapy tablets. And people don't want a dog that is sick. They want a healthy dog'. Bob's sarcastic comments were not lost on Winston, who looked at him as if questioning his sanity.

An alarm bell sounded and the food dispensers in each of the separate kennels dispensed a set amount of food for the dogs. Winston turned to look at the very basic dog food that was on offer. It was full of corn, soy and wheat and it was nutrient-deficient for canines. Winston knew his stomach was adversely affected by the food, but he also knew that Bob would not offer him any alternatives, so it was either eat it or go hungry. Winston looked back at Bob in what appeared to be disgust and then began to eat the measly food on offer.

Bob laughed out loud in front of Winston, and then went on his way to terrorise another poor soul. Winston begrudgingly ate the food, knowing that he would pay the cost later on. He hadn't been regular since he had arrived, and he knew there was an acute difference between the food served at the shelter and the food at his previous home. Even the water at the shelter somehow tasted different - maybe it was less clean.

After he had eaten, Winston sat down on his blanket. He began to clean himself, first licking his paws and then licking his nose again and again. He then rubbed his eyes with his paws to try to get the sleep out of them. As he lay there cleaning himself, he knew that he had another fun packed day of sitting, lying and listening to the other dogs barking and whining.

A short while later, Winston could hear someone arrive. It was a lady and she was talking to Bob about something. She sounded friendly. He wished he could see out of his cage; he would love to be able to see what was going on. Who was this visitor? And was she after a Pug? He hoped so.

Winston could hear two sets of footsteps approaching. He was sure that they would stop before they got as far as his kennel, but they didn't. Slowly but surely, the footsteps continued and as they did, dogs barked and jumped up and down when they saw Bob and his visitor walk by, trying to grab their attention. Winston continued to look down at the floor, expecting to be overlooked again. The footsteps stopped, and Winston felt as if he was being watched. He slowly raised his eyes and looked up. And to his surprise, he saw Bob and his visitor looking down at him.

It was a lady, as he had suspected. And Winston thought she had very kind eyes. She looked down at him and tears welled up in her eyes. She wiped them away with her sleeve and continued to look endearingly at him. Winston thought that she had a friendly face. He could also tell that she was smiling through the tears, which was a good sign. She looked slightly overweight, and she had curly dark brown hair, brown eyes, a fuller face with chubby cheeks, and a small mouth. Her cheeks looked red from the cold outside. And she wore a knitted Christmas jumper, green corduroy pants, and some wellington boots. She also wore gloves and a big overcoat that was open at the front.

'He's lovely', said Alison to Bob. 'Just perfect'.

'You know about his medical history, don't you?' asked Bob.

'Yes, I read on your website that he is in remission for cancer of the lymph nodes, and that he has had it on more than one occasion. So I am well aware of what I am taking on....'

'That's right. You will need to take comprehensive pet insurance out on him. And it won't be cheap. He has been very sick in the past'.

'The poor little guy', said Alison while looking down at his ever so sad face. 'We will take care of him. Me and my daughter. He will be loved'.

'That's good to know', said Bob. Whether he was genuine was up for debate. 'Lets go and have a chat in my office. Discuss the price and documents that need to be signed'.

'Before I go, I would like to hold him'.

'Of course', said Bob who opened the cage door of the kennel and knelt down to pick up Winston. As he did, Winston barked his disapproval. But once he was handed over to Alison, the barking stopped and instead Winston whined very quietly. He also seemed to be shaking. Alison thought that it must be quite stressful for dogs when strangers came into their life; she knew that Winston was probably wary of her. She held him in her arms and gently stroked his back. The whining seemed to stop and Winston seemed to relax. Alison kissed him on the cheek and a tear slowly ran down her face. She then gave him a big cuddle and cried some more. For his part, Winston snuggled up to her and licked her ear lobe. He sniffed her cheek and he felt secure and comforted in her arms. He had been starved of human affection over the last 3 months, so he was glad of any chance he got to be cuddled and held.

'I wish I could take him home now. He looks so forlorn. Like the weight of the world is on his shoulders', said Alison. Bob grunted his agreement. As she continued to hold him, she realised how light he was. She had expected him to be much heavier. 'How come he is so light?'

'He's smaller than the average pug. I believe that is the reason why', said Bob. However, Alison suspected that the dogs weren't fed well. Judging by the state of the place, the dogs were probably in dire need of a good wash or bath, and were probably all malnourished. Alison had already decided that she was going to complain to the authorities about this dog shelter, but she wanted to wait until she had secured Winston before she did. She didn't want anything to scupper her chances of receiving him.

'Goodbye Winston, I will come back to pick you up soon', said Alison as she carefully placed him back in his kennel. Bob shut the cage door. Alison waved at Winston, who looked up at her with the saddest eyes that she had ever seen. As Bob and Alison made their way to the office, Winston watched them until they were no longer in sight. As they walked away, the other dogs suddenly started barking and whimpering and whining, looking for some well-needed attention from Bob and his visitor.

Winston felt very sad because he had hoped that the lady was going to take him away from this godforsaken place. But she had left him like all the rest did. Winston didn't know if he would ever leave the shelter. He sat down on his blanket and curled up into a ball.

BECKY'S PROMISE

Since her visit to the dog shelter, Alison had busied herself making a coffee and walnut cake in the kitchen. Trying her best not to eat too many walnuts, she had managed to get most of the ingredients into the cake tin, and it was now baking in the oven. The smell emanating from the kitchen was heavenly. And it was not lost on Becky and her home school tutor, who was visiting that afternoon to go through some of the things that Alison found difficult to teach Becky. To placate them both, Alison had opened her tin of goodies and had given Becky and her tutor a piece of homemade chocolate caramel shortbread.

While waiting for the tutor to go and for the cake to bake, Alison had looked out over her back garden. She watched as a robin red breast flew from branch to branch picking up little berries along the way. The snow kept on falling, and as she looked out, it got noticeably heavier and thicker. It began to lay thick on the ground, and Alison felt all cosy inside as she looked out over a cold frosty winter landscape. Alison and her daughter lived in a little cottage, on the outskirts of town, and they had always loved living there. It felt like they lived out of town as their house stood on its own, surrounded by trees and farmland. Yet only 400 metres away were the outskirts of the main town. And the main grocery stores and shops were a mere five minute drive away. Alison had always thought she had the best of both worlds. A rural location in an urban setting.

Now that Christmas was almost upon them, she wanted to make it a holiday that Becky would never forget. Because everything she did was for Becky. She wanted to make amends for past Christmases, when Becky had been sick one year after the other. It had been a tough few years. Notwithstanding Becky's health, they had both had to endure the premature death of Alison's husband and Becky's father, Stephen. He had been out for a walk with their family dog and had suffered a sudden and devastating heart attack. With no one to help him in the woods, he had lain there in severe pain. The dog, Shelley, had remained with her owner, and had licked his cheeks in an attempt to wake him up. But he died before a passer-by found him. Both Alison and Becky had been heartbroken and still were; they missed him terribly. It seemed that Shelley had also missed him, because it wasn't long before she died without explanation at the relatively young age of 9 for a border collie.

Alison looked out of the window at the wintry scene outside. They had experienced a few difficult years recently and they certainly weren't out of the woods yet. But Alison hoped that their new dog, Winston, might signal a new beginning. Maybe he was a beacon of hope. She had made the arrangements with Bob Fletcher to pick him up in a couple of days' time. And she was looking forward to seeing him again very much; and she couldn't wait to tell Becky the good news.

Once Becky's tutor had gone, Alison came through to the sitting room and joined Becky on the sofa. She brought through a tray with two mugs on it consisting of Becky's favourite drink, Ovaltine, and a coffee for herself.

'Becky, I have some really good news that I have been dying to share with you', said Alison. Her face could not contain her excitement, and Becky looked at her with wonder in her eyes.

'What is it, Mom?' asked Becky.

'It's the best news ever! I have bought you an early Christmas present'.

'Oh wow! What is it?' said Becky.

'Well, I never know what to get you. But this time, it was a no-brainer. You are gonna love it', said Alison, who handed Becky a small gift wrapped up in Christmas paper.

Ripping it open to reveal a dog collar with the name 'Winston' on it, Becky was speechless. With her mouth wide open, she looked at her mother aghast. Alison smiled warmly back to her.

'A - a - a - a- dog!?' said Becky. Alison nodded and Becky jumped up off the sofa and as high as she could in the air. 'Yay, yay, yay, yay, yay!!'

Alison looked at her daughter and tears of joy started to form in her eyes. She tried to wipe them away, but more came. Becky's face had lit up when she had seen the dog collar, and she had looked radiant for the first time in months, Alison thought. It had lit a switch in Becky that had been turned off for months if not years. Her 9 year old daughter jumped back on to the sofa, cross legged and eager to know more. Her sandy hair fell out of its ponytail and dropped down on either side of her face. Her pale complexion had suddenly dissipated, and the colour in her cheeks had returned. Her blue eyes shone like diamonds, and that smile - a smile that Alison had dreamt about seeing again - had returned.

Becky said, 'So Mom, tell me all about it. What kind of dog is it? I guess it's a boy cos it's called Winston'.

Alison smiled and looked lovingly at Becky. 'Yes, he is the most beautiful Pug I have ever seen. Sad eyes, but a lovely light brown coat of fur, and a cheeky face. He is quite small and he's only 4 years old. And he needs a home. He is currently in the dog shelter'.

'Awww, poor Winston', said Becky. 'How could anyone stick him in a dog shelter?'

'Well, there's one thing you need to know about him. Unfortunately, he has had lymphoma cancer in the past. He is in remission, but it may return again. So he might be sick in the future. We just don't know'.

'Oh, poor Winston. I want to give him the biggest cuddle ever, and tell him everything is going to be okay. He must be sad in that shelter. I can't wait to meet him. When is he coming here?'

Alison looked endearingly at her daughter. 'The day after tomorrow. I will pick him up first thing on Saturday morning. We need to get prepared for his arrival. I have to pick up some new things for him.

Blankets, dog food, treats, a bone, somewhere for him
to sleep - a dog bed, and water and food bowls too.
And probably some other things that I can't think of
right now'.

'We are going to love him so much. He will be
spoiled so badly!' said Becky. She smiled from ear to
ear; she could not keep smiling. It had made her year,
and she couldn't believe that Winston would be here
in time for Christmas. She was overjoyed. 'Thankyou
Mom. It's the best Christmas present ever!' Becky
got up and gave her mother a big cuddle and kiss.

'I am pleased that you are so happy. But just
remember, a dog is for life, not just for Christmas. I
didn't want to buy you a dog for Christmas, but when
I saw a picture of Winston, my heart melted'.

'Have you got a photo of him?' asked Becky
impatiently. 'Please let me see, let me see....' Alison
turned her smart phone on and found a picture of him,
walked over to Becky and showed it to her.

'He is gorgeous. What a cutie! I love him
already!' said Becky.

Alison endearingly ran her hand down Becky's
face, then sat back down on the sofa. 'You are gonna
love him. He is such a cutie. He was a bit wary when

I met him, but I think it won't take long to gain his trust. He seems like a very loving dog'.

'This has made my year! I can't believe it!' said Becky, who got up off the sofa and started dancing around the sitting room. The joy in her heart knew no bounds. She had missed having canine company around, and someone to make a fuss over and look after. She couldn't wait for Saturday morning to arrive. She knew one thing - that Winston would be overwhelmed by the love that she was going to give him.

'Tomorrow is 'Get Ready' day. We need to make this place dog friendly, and ensure that we have everything in place for his arrival. I will make a list tonight and we can go shopping tomorrow', said Alison.

Becky nodded and jumped up high in the air, shouting 'Yay! Yay! Yay!'

WINSTON'S ARRIVAL

It was Saturday morning. Bob Fletcher made his way from home into town in his Cherokee Pick Up Truck. As he drove through the snow flurries, he wished he was still in his bed. He couldn't be bothered to look after those pesky dogs. As far as he was concerned, they were more trouble than they were worth. He had had just about enough of their whining, barking and causing a mess. It hadn't occurred to him yet that he was in the wrong job, and that the dog shelter needed someone who actually genuinely cared for animals.

As his truck entered the main street in town, he could see the Christmas lights hanging from tree to tree, and lamppost to lamppost. The snow continued to lie on the ground, and Bob suspected that he might have to dig himself out of the dog shelter car park if it got much worse. He parked up outside, got out of his truck and opened up the dog shelter.

As he walked in, some of the dogs barked and some others whined.

'Ah, shut up!' Bob shouted. 'You're just a bunch of cretins!'

The barking continued as did the whining. Bob got a hold of a spade that he used to clean out the kennels, and he raised it in the air with his left hand and tapped it against his right hand. 'If you don't shut up soon, I will do more than just clean out your kennels with this spade!' He then smashed the blade of the spade against the wall. Most of the dogs who had been making a noise stopped suddenly.

Bob walked up and down the corridor of the dog shelter, looking left and right at his charges. When he reached Winston, he looked down at the sad looking creature that was still half asleep lying in his blanket, and said, 'You're escaping the madness today. Shame! I didn't think anyone would take you on. I mean, how long have you got to live? One month? Two? Your cancer will come back, no doubt'.

Winston looked up at Bob reluctantly but his face did not flicker. It was as if Winston knew exactly what Bob was saying, and couldn't be bothered to respond to such nonsense. Instead, Winston reverted his gaze and began to use his paws to clean the sleep from his eyes.

Bob continued on his way and started to clean the kennels. When he got to Sable, the Labrador's kennel, he found a bit of a mess. Sable obviously had an upset stomach and she hadn't made it to her toilet in time, and had left a present for Bob on the floor. He was not amused at all. He opened the cage door and walked inside the kennel area. As he did, with his back to the corridor, he began to clean up the mess.

'You stupid dog! Look what you have done! Don't you realise that it's Muggins here who has got to clean your mess up. You dirty little mutt!' shouted Bob, who then struck Sable across the face with his hand. It wasn't a tap either; it was a forceful slap. Sable whimpered in pain.

'Ah, shut up! You deserve it!' shouted Bob. 'Don't do it again! Or you will get more of the same!'

About twenty seconds later, Bob felt someone's presence behind him. He suddenly turned around and saw Alison standing there.

'Hello Bob. I am here to pick up little Winston this morning', she said.

'Ah, hi Alison. I was just cleaning out the kennels. I will be with you shortly. You have already signed most of the documents, so it's just a case of handing him over to you and giving you his release papers'.

'Thanks Bob', said Alison. She walked on past Bob, and as she walked along, she looked at the mostly sad eyes that were staring at her from each kennel. She wished she could take them all home. She hoped that they would all find suitable family homes soon. This dog shelter was not a nice place for them, she thought.

She arrived at Winston's kennel, and looked down at the little guy who was still half asleep on his blanket. He opened his eyes and saw Alison looking at him. He realised that she had come back for him. He got up suddenly and ran towards the front of the kennel, his face pressed against the cage door, staring at her intently. She knelt down and put her fingers through the cage, and Winston began to lick them.

'I've come to take you home, Winston. I can't wait to introduce you to Becky. She is gonna absolutely adore you. I am sure of it! You look so cute and loving. Not long now and I will have you out of here'.

It was as if Winston understood every word because he started to dance around the cage and move his head from side to side. He kept on looking back at

Alison, as if he was worried in case she disappeared when he wasn't looking at her. Bob walked down the corridor and opened the cage door to the kennel. As he did, Winston came running to the front and Alison picked him up in her arms and gave him the biggest cuddle ever.

'Oh, Winston. I think I love you already!' she said, cradling him in her arms. She then kissed him and he licked her cheek. She then carried him along the corridor, following Bob into his office to sign some final release documents. As Alison walked along, Winston looked at the kennels on his left and right and finally got to see what some of the other dogs looked like. Some barked at him for attention; others just stared at him. As they walked past Sable, both Alison and Winston looked at her. She was cowering in the corner of her kennel and appeared to be shaking ever so slightly. Alison whispered to Sable, 'Don't worry. I will help you'.

Five minutes later, Alison carried Winston out of the dog shelter. As they walked out of the main door, Winston got a shock. His eyes were nearly blinded by the white of the snow all around him. Coming from a dingy and dark dog shelter, the contrast couldn't have been more stark. He closed his eyes and reopened them a few times to try to readjust to the blinding light. As he did, he felt flakes of snow falling on his beautiful fur coat, and a couple of flakes dropped on his nose, making it feel itchy. He sniffled a couple of times, but he couldn't stop the sneeze that was about to happen. He closed his eyes and let out an almighty sneeze. Alison, who was holding him in her arms, got a shock. 'Ah, Bless you Winston', she said.

Winston looked all around him as Alison plonked him down on the passenger seat of her car and she got into the drivers side. He could see people all dressed up warm walking around the town centre streets. The snow was falling all around them, and he could see Christmas lights lit up everywhere. He saw a couple of people with dogs walk by. One dog was being held by her owner and he recognised who it was instantly. Maisie!!

He yelped and barked at her, but realised that she probably couldn't hear him from inside the car. He was so pleased that he had seen her again. Maybe they would meet up again soon.

As Alison drove off, he looked back at the dog shelter. *Good riddance to bad rubbish,* he thought, as the shelter disappeared out of view. He was so pleased to have left, and so relieved that he would not have to see Bob Fletcher again. As they drove along, Winston the Pug looked from one side of the car to the next. He was so inquisitive. He had been cocooned in that place for too long. He was now able to see what was going on outside; he had missed it so much. Kids carrying their sledges to the nearby field, families going Christmas shopping, old men going into the local hostelries for a beer or two, people on their way to work or doing errands, and the hustle and bustle of the Christmas market where people were sampling mulled wine, cheese and biscuits, and buying gifts for their loved ones. Winston was fascinated by the world outside.

Within a few minutes, they had driven out of town and were now approaching Alison and Becky's little cottage. Waiting at the window in the sitting room was Becky and Louise, who was looking after Becky while Alison had gone out. Becky saw her mother's car arrive home and she could see a little dog inside, jumping up and down inquisitively in the passenger seat.

Alison picked up her things and then picked up Winston, and got out of the car. As she walked towards the front door, it opened and Becky stood at the entrance. She looked straight at Winston and began to cry; they were tears of joy.

'Oh, Mom. He is beautiful. So cute!' said Becky. Alison handed him to Becky who cradled him

in her arms and kissed him a few times on his head.
Winston was loving all of the attention, and he began
to lick Becky's hand, and he turned and kissed her on
the cheek.

'Oh Winston. You are perfect. Just perfect!'
Becky then walked into the sitting room, holding him
close to her chest. She sat down on the sofa and
stroked him gently.

Louise walked into the kitchen, where Alison
was.

'How did it go, Alison? No problems?' asked
Louise.

'As far as bringing Winston back, it went really
well. The process was smooth; I signed the release
documents, as did Bob. But Louise, that place is
absolutely awful. The dogs are not looked after
properly. They are being mistreated'.

'How do you know?' asked Louise.

'I could hear Bob shouting at someone so I
walked into the shelter quietly. As I did, I realised
that he was shouting at one of the poor dogs. I think
she had soiled her kennel. Anyway, I took out my
phone without thinking and started filming. As I did, I

found Bob in one of the kennels. He was castigating this poor dog and then suddenly he slapped her across the face! I was astounded'.

Louise put her hand to her mouth in shock. 'That's awful! The evil pig! What did you do?'

'I am ashamed to say that I filmed it and then quickly put my phone back into my pocket before he saw me', said Alison. 'I didn't want to jeopardize getting little Winston. I wanted to make sure I had him safe and sound at home first. I've been meaning to complain about that place all along, but now I will have to send my video footage to the ASPCA. I feel really guilty; maybe I should have confronted him there and then', said Alison.

'You did the right thing, Alison. As you say, he could have stopped you getting Winston. And he could have taken it out on Winston later behind closed doors. I would have done the same thing. But I can see your dilemma. Don't forget - you had a split second to make a decision. You didn't have the luxury of time. As long as he has no comeback on you anymore, I would report him as soon as you can'.

Alison sighed deeply. 'I will. He can't treat animals like that and get away with it'.

'Maybe you could speak to your old friend. What was his name again? Roger? Doesn't he work for the ASPCA now?' said Louise.

'Ah, yes, you're right. Good shout! I will contact him. I just hope Bob doesn't try to take revenge on me....he's a bit of a loose cannon'.

'If he does, everyone in the town would make sure justice is done - and get him apprehended. Don't worry, Alison', said Louise, who then patted her friend on the shoulder. 'He will make his situation even worse if he tries anything. We would run him out of town!'

Alison looked worried, but remained resolute. 'Yeah, I can't not report him. The poor dogs. As I walked along the corridor, all I could see was sad eyes staring at me from either side. It was heartbreaking. I have to do something for all those dogs. I just hope the authorities don't end up closing the shelter down and euthanizing them all'.

It was Louise's turn to look worried. She furrowed her brow, looked out of the window at the snow falling in the back garden, and contemplated if that was a possibility. 'If that happens, we will try and re-house all the dogs before the authorities get their hands on them. Let's wait and see what happens'.

Just then, the doorbell rang. Alison looked worried. Just as Louise started to make her way to the front door, Becky came flying out of the sitting room carrying little Winston and ran up to the front door. She opened it quickly.

'Good morning, Becky' said the postman. 'And what have you got there?' He pointed to the little Pug in her arms.

'It's Winston. He's just arrived. Isn't he a cutie?' said Becky.

'He sure is. He's a bonny lad. I'm used to dogs biting me and barking at me. Makes a nice change to have a nice natured dog. It looks like he wouldn't say Boo to a goose'.

'Yeah, I think he's really kind and gentle. I don't think he'll bite you'.

'That's good to know. Now, is your Mom in? I need her to sign for a letter'.

Alison stood in the hallway and heard the postman. She walked up to the front door, and shuffled past Becky and Winston. 'Good morning Peter. I'll sign for it'.

'I was just saying to Becky, what a nice dog you have', said Peter.

'Yeah. He is one in a million. I love him already, and I hardly know him'. Alison signed for the letter, and Peter said his goodbyes.

'Goodbye Peter the Postman', said Becky as he walked away. He waved back to her and as he did, Winston yelped once. Becky laughed and gave him a kiss on the cheek.

CHRISTMAS DECORATIONS

It was Sunday morning. Becky had hardly slept because she was so excited with the new addition to the family. She kept on waking up and looking at Winston who was asleep in the dog bed that was on the floor in her room. She kept on looking just to make sure that he was okay; and just to reassure herself that he wasn't something that she had dreamt; that he was in fact real. Each time she woke up, she could see him lying curled up in a ball. His eyes were closed and she thought she could hear him snoring very lightly. He looked so serene and happy, now that he was away from that dog shelter.

Becky looked at the clock. It was now 6.30am. She didn't want to wait any longer, so she got up and when she walked to the bathroom, her footsteps woke Winston up. On her way back to her bed, she picked him up and took him to bed with her.

'Morning Winston', she said. 'You had a really long sleep. Not like me. I could hardly sleep'.

He looked at her through sleepy eyes, and then he lay down on the pillow next to her.

'Aww, Winston. You are still tired. You must have needed that sleep. Maybe you never got any sleep in that awful place - the shelter. Well, you don't need to worry. You are staying here for good. No one can take you away from me'. She kissed him on the face and lay down next to him on the adjoining pillow, so that they were face to face. 'Mom doesn't want you in my bed, but she can't stop you. I will let you sleep in here tonight. I know you wanted to last night, but Mom insisted you use the dog bed'.

Winston started to lick his paws and then looked at her with his dreamy and sad eyes. Becky went up close to him and smelt his head. 'You are so clean. Bet you are so pleased we bathed you last night. I think you needed a proper bath. They didn't look after you very well at the shelter, did they? Well, you are home now. There's nothing to worry about. And you smell nice!'

He looked at her and yawned. She cuddled him again, and he licked her face in return. He was so much happier, now that he was in a lovely house with lovely people. He hoped that this was his new family. He had already grown attached to them both; it didn't take long for Pugs to become loyal and affectionate towards their new owners. And Winston was no different.

'So, Winston. Mom told me all about your cancer treatment', said Becky. Winston raised his head off the pillow as if he had understood what she was saying. 'Well, I just want you to know that you are in remission and that hopefully it won't come back. And there is something you should know'. Becky looked at him with a tear in her eye. 'I also had the same cancer as you. I had Hodgkins Lymphoma. But they gave me chemotherapy. Not the tablets that you got. I got it from a tube that they put into my body. And I felt really poorly. Mom says that dogs don't get sick from chemotherapy. But humans do'.

Winston looked at her inquisitively, as if he was paying attention to every word that she was saying. 'But I am in remission now, just like you. I got the all clear only a week ago. But I gotta remain at home. I can't go back to school. They want to make sure I am completely healthy before I am allowed back. And I do worry a little about going back. I have lost some of my long hair and it's patchy now. And I look a lot paler. I have also lost a lot of weight. You wouldn't know that cos you haven't seen a picture of me before. But I was a lot heavier before my treatment'.

He got up and moved over to lick her face gently. She smiled as he did, and put her arm around him and gave him a cuddle. He looked at her with those big wonderful eyes and it made her feel so happy that he was all hers. She squeezed him ever so gently. 'I'm gonna dress you up for Christmas. You definitely need a Christmas jumper. I am gonna get you one for your Christmas present. You will look really smart with one on', she said.

A few hours later, Winston was in his element. In the sitting room, he was surrounded by toys, decorations and a massive undecorated Christmas tree in the corner of the room. He jumped up and down and used his nose to flick the toys in the air as he ran around the sitting room floor. Becky stood by him and watched as he was having the time of his life. After playing with a couple of toy Santas, he picked up some tinsel and began to run with it in his mouth, so that it trailed behind him as he ran. He made a grunting noise as he exerted a lot of effort to run back and forwards. Becky laughed at him as he was in his element - he was so happy, and so was she. Originally she had asked him to help her with the decorations. However, far from being a help, he was more of a hindrance as he kept on stealing the decorations as if they were his property. Again and again, Becky fell about laughing. She hadn't had so much fun in years, she thought.

'Winston, bring back that golden tinsel. I want to start decorating the tree', said a laughing Becky. 'You are so naughty. But I could never ever be cross with you. You are too cute by far!' As soon as she said that, his face appeared from behind the back of the sofa. He still had the golden tinsel in his mouth and was looking guilty.

'There you are! Where have you been? Winston? Where have you been?' she said. He slowly walked towards her and dropped the tinsel on the ground in front of her. It appeared that he was sick of playing with it, and instead he picked up a toy elf with his mouth and then threw it in the air, allowing it to drop on the floor. Becky grabbed a hold of the tinsel before he could run away with it again, and she draped it around the Christmas tree. She looked back and he was gone again. She could hear him behind the sofa, making grunting noises, and she smiled. She had never smiled so much; her mouth was aching.

In the kitchen, her mother Alison was on the phone to her friend Roger Caffrey, who worked for the American Society for the Prevention of Cruelty to Animals (ASPCA). She asked him if he could help, and he said he would try his best.

'I have sent you the video and a statement that I have written. That guy should not be looking after dogs', said Alison on the phone.

'I agree. From what you have said, it sounds like a hell hole. We need to investigate his behaviour, but more importantly the welfare of the dogs. I will let you know how we get on', said Roger on the other end.

Alison bit her lip, and then said, 'Roger, what happens if they have to close the shelter? I couldn't bear it if they ended up euthanizing all the dogs. It would break my heart, and I would feel guilty somehow'. She then started to grip the kitchen table with her fingers as she waited for his response.

'I can assure you. That is always a last resort. We look to re-home them where possible'.

'I want to help re-home them if you can't find a suitable dog shelter...I would try my best to find suitable homes for the dogs here - in town', said Alison. Her fingers had turned white from gripping the table so hard, such was her anxiety about the whole situation.

Roger tried to reassure her on the phone. 'I will keep in touch and let you know how we get on. Don't worry. You have done the right thing. Thanks for letting us know'.

A couple of minutes later, Alison walked through to the sitting room and was shocked by what she saw. She found a tree that was barely decorated, a daughter who was laughing silly, and a little pug called Winston who was over-excited, playing with an assortment of Christmas decorations. Alison stood in the doorway with her hands on her hips, with a slightly annoyed look on her face. She wanted to tell Becky off, but then thought better of it.

'You are both very naughty', she said to Becky and Winston. 'You should both be ashamed of yourselves!' Becky looked across at her mother and looked guilty as if she had done wrong. But Alison began to laugh out loud and then shook her head slowly. 'How could I be mad at you both? It's impossible. I'm just pleased that you are having so much fun. And those decorations are past it anyway. We've needed new ones for years'.

Just then, Winston picked up some red tinsel and started to run around with it. He ran in circles, getting all tangled up with the tinsel. And then he ran with it in his mouth from one end of the room to the other. Alison looked at him as if he was mad. Beckly laughed uncontrollably. Alison began to chuckle looking at both of them; she tried to stifle her laughter but couldn't stop.

'You are incorrigible, Winston! You've only been here barely 24 hours and already you are causing mayhem. What a tinker!' said Alison. As soon as she said it, Winston suddenly stopped playing and dropped the tinsel. He looked up at Alison as if he knew he had been castigated for being naughty. His sad-looking eyes made Alison melt, and she said, 'I'm sorry Winston. Keep on playing!' She picked up the tinsel from the ground and then threw it in the air. On its way down, Winston caught it in his mouth and began to run around again, as if he realised she had given him the green light to continue playing.

'I swear that little guy knows what we are saying. He's very intelligent', said Alison.

'Yeah, he sure is! I love him already, Mom. He is the greatest!' said Becky.

Alison smiled warmly. 'I'm glad....I'm really glad'. She looked out of the sitting room window at the thick snow that was falling down. The front garden was blanketed with snow, and the height of the snow on the ground was beginning to rise steadily. 'We're gonna be snowed in shortly', she said.

Becky ran over to the window and looked out at the wintry scene. Winston ran after her and tried to jump up onto the window ledge to see what she was looking at, but failed miserably. She looked down at him, laughed, and picked him up so that he could look outside. He seemed really interested and amazed by the snow.

'Becky, you do know that Pugs can't go in the snow. They don't like the cold, so Winston wouldn't appreciate going out in that. He's a fair weather dog'.

'I thought so. He looks so fragile. I would hate to give him a cold or dog flu', replied Becky as she plonked him down on the window ledge and began to stroke his head. He looked up at where the snow was coming from, and then he looked around the front garden and the road outside, which was even quieter than normal.

As she turned to walk away, Winston turned around with her. But he was still stuck on the window ledge. He looked down at the floor, debating whether he could jump or not. He was wary, and was in two minds whether to jump. As Becky walked away, he looked at her, as if asking her to let him down. He let out a short yelp, and she came running back to pick him up.

'Awww, I am sorry Winston. I didn't mean to leave you high and dry', she said. She picked him up and dropped him back down on the floor. Turning to her mother, she asked, 'How is your book getting on, Mom?'

'I've finished it. Louise is going to proof read it for me, and then I will publish it online. It's book 5 in the series. I think it might do as well as the last one. If it did, I would be over the moon'.

'Oh, that's great Mom. I hope so'. Becky returned to decorating the Christmas tree, and continued to wrap some of the tinsel around the tree, and put some of the baubles up. Meanwhile, Alison disentangled the Christmas lights on the dining room table, out of dog's reach, and then brought them back into the sitting room. As she approached Becky and the tree, Becky said, 'Is it okay if I buy Winston a jumper for Christmas?' And she whispered the last part of the sentence, 'jumper for Christmas', in case Winston heard her.

'Yes, I think that will be a great idea. It will keep him extra warm too'. Alison put her hand on Becky's shoulder and squeezed it gently. 'What a kind girl you are. Always thinking of others'.

And as they continued to decorate the tree and the snow fell down outside, both Alison and Becky felt as if life couldn't get any better. They had a beautiful new dog, a cosy and happy home, and a great support network around them. Alison could have pinched herself.

UNWELCOME VISITOR

A few days past, and Becky and Alison got to know their new Pug friend a whole lot better. They got to know his foibles, his habits, behaviours, manners, and his character. And so far, they were mightily impressed. Winston was such a caring dog; loyal, affectionate, trusting, friendly, and loving. He wouldn't leave Becky's side - ever. It was like he was glued to her. And she in turn adored him. By now, he had managed to wind his way to sleep in Becky's bed. Her mother had not approved, but there wasn't much she could do. Both Becky and Winston were happy with the arrangement!

It was Wednesday morning. Winston licked Becky's face to wake her up. He looked at her inquisitively and lay back down next to her. She opened her eyes slowly and looked across at him. 'Good morning Winston. You are very naughty. Waking me up, and now it looks like you are going back to sleep. You cheeky boy!' She stroked his face gently and she patted his head. She looked out of the window in her bedroom to reveal a snowy scene outside. More snow had fallen last night and it looked very thick on the ground.

'I wonder if Mom will let me play outside today. Or maybe go for a walk. I would love to walk in the snow', she said to Winston. He looked back at her as if he was taking in everything she was saying. 'But I don't know if she will allow you to come out with us. It might be too cold for you. And I don't want you to catch a cold'.

At that same time, Alison was woken up by a phone call on her mobile, which was on her bedside table in her bedroom. Still half asleep, she reached for the phone without looking, and initially struggled to find it. Eventually, she got a hold of it, checked the screen that told her Louise was calling, and answered it straight away.

'Hey Alison, I'm really sorry. You are probably still asleep. But I had to let you know. Turn on your TV and go to Channel 11. You won't believe it', said Louise.

Alison quickly grabbed her bedroom TV's remote control, pressed the power button and navigated to Channel 11. 'I hope this is good news, L?'

'Yeah, I think it's very good news. An early Christmas present', replied Louise.

After a few seconds, she found Channel 11. 'Oh my God!' said Alison.

'I couldn't believe it either. I saw it half an hour ago and knew they were going to show it again now. They've arrested Bob. The ASPCA were involved, and so were the local police'.

'This is great news. But what about the dogs in the shelter?'

'The news report said that the ASPCA has found new homes for them in some neighbouring shelters. They said a couple were bought by the local police officers who helped in the arrest. I am just so happy that Bob can't lay a finger on them anymore. Even if they don't put him in jail, he won't be able to work in dog shelters again. He'll probably get fined too'.

Alison was so relieved. She sighed deeply. 'Oh, Louise. It's great news. I am so pleased that the dogs are okay. I felt terrible leaving them in there. But I think this was the best way to do it'.

'He would have probably stopped you buying Winston for sure, if you had brought it up with him when you last saw him. You did the right thing,

Alison. And you gave all those dogs a wonderful Christmas present. At this rate, they stand a very good chance of seeing next Christmas. It might have been a very different story otherwise', said Louise.

'I just hope Bob doesn't try and take revenge on me, or something. He might be unhinged for all we know'.

Louise remained silent on the phone for a couple of seconds. 'Just be vigilant when you go out. But I think he won't try anything because he would just make things a whole lot worse'.

Later that morning, Becky busied herself with some homework while Alison did some household chores such as washing and ironing. As Becky studied, she kept on looking out of the window at the beautiful snowscape. She longed to go out for a walk; to get some fresh air and to trudge in the snow. Alison made cups of tea for them both and brought a cup into the dining room where Becky was busy working.

'Thanks Mom. I was wondering if we could go out for a walk soon. I would love to walk in the snow. I will wrap up really well'.

'Okay, Becky. I think that's a great idea. We can walk along the old country lane. It will be beautiful at the top of the hill. The views of the valley will be amazing. Remember what it was like last year?' said Alison.

'Yes, it was great....How about we go before lunch?'

'Okay, after this cup of tea then'.

'And I will carry Winston along. He is always looking outside. I think he would love to go out', said Becky. She said it quickly in the hope that her mother would forget the conversation they had a few days ago about this same subject.

'Becky. What I have told you about Winston?' asked Alison sternly. 'You know that it's too cold for Winston to go out in the snow. And I don't think you could carry him all that way. You would have to put him down and he would be frozen'.

'Ah, Mom!' said Becky, looking very distressed at what her mother had just said. 'But how are we gonna go out? We can't leave him on his own'.

'We can leave him on his own. In fact, this will be his first test - let's see how he copes when we leave him in the house alone. He has to get used to it, because there will be times when we have to leave him on his own', said Alison in her motherly voice. 'That's why we have been doing the Leave & Return scenario with him. To make him realise that there will be times when we will leave him on his own'.

Becky sulked for a few seconds. Her face dropped to the floor at the thought of leaving poor Winston on his own. She looked down at her feet, where Winston lay. Feeling her stare, he looked up at her with the saddest of sad eyes. The eyes that could melt a million hearts. And she felt a bit upset about leaving him to fend for himself. After a few more seconds, he lay back down on the carpet, all fours legs outstretched.

'It's good for him to be on his own. He's got to realise that we go out from time to time. You will be going back to school after Christmas, so he will have to get used to that too. And so will you!'

Becky smiled. 'I can't wait to go back to school. To see all my friends. It's been ages since I was last there'.

'Now that you are better, you can go back. And little Winston will have to get used to it. But he will realise that you aren't leaving him for good. Just think about where he used to live and where he lives now. Our home is a palace compared to the dog shelter', said Alison, again in her best motherly voice.

Both mother and daughter finished off their cups of tea, got changed into their warm winter gear, and put their wellington boots on. Winston watched on with curiosity. They both looked a picture. Overcoats, gloves, woolly hats, boots, and waterproof trousers. They were all kitted out for the snowy and frosty conditions outside. As they stood at the front door, Winston was hanging around them and sniffing the clothes that they were wearing. And he pressed his paws down on the front of Becky's wellington boots again and again.

'We are off for a walk, Winston. I am sorry. Mom says you can't go in the sitting room or dining room, but you can walk between the front door, kitchen and laundry room. But don't worry. We won't be long', said Becky. Winston appeared to nod. 'Did he just nod?' she asked her Mom.

'Don't be silly', Alison replied. 'He's not that clever!'

'I don't know. I think he did'. They opened the front door and Winston tried to follow them outside.

But they closed the door so he couldn't follow them. 'Bye Winston. I won't be long. I promise'.

The fresh air was so refreshing after Becky had been cooped up in the little cottage for a week or so. The winter sunshine helped to take some of the chill out of the air, but it was still bitterly cold. As they walked along their drive to the road outside, they realised how deep the snow was. When Becky put her foot down, it sunk about a foot and a half into the snow.

'Wow, Mom. It's so deep. It's amazing'.

When they got to the road, they started to walk up it. As they did, Becky looked back at the cottage. She couldn't see Winston, but she hoped that he was okay. They continued up the road until they reached the track that would take them to the top of the hill. It was slow progress because the snow was so deep, and Becky had to exert a lot of energy just to put one foot in front of the other.

'Just take your time, Becky. You're still recuperating after being in hospital. Remember that'.

'I know, Mom'.

'And don't worry about little Winston. He will be fine. He has to get used to it'.

They continued on their way, and made slow progress up the hillside. Someone was watching them as they walked on.

Meanwhile, Winston was still at the front door. He waited there a while for them to return. He expected that they might come back imminently. After a few more minutes, he realised that they must have gone. He then wandered back and forwards between the front door and the kitchen. He was able to walk into the laundry room from the kitchen, and from there he could see out of the double patio doors into the back garden. He looked out of the windows for a while, and could see little Robin Red Breasts either playing together or fighting together. He watched them for a while, and then wandered back into the hallway and sat down on a rug which had been brought through for him. He began to lick and clean himself, using his paws to clean his ears and his eyes. He then licked his paws and his brown fur coat.

Then, he heard a sound outside. He looked up and his eyes darted from left to right. He listened again; there was someone outside. He got up and ran to the front door. He couldn't sense that anyone was behind the door. So he trotted quickly to the kitchen, and then went through to the laundry room. As he skipped into the room, he got the shock of his life. At the double patio doors was a man. But not just any man. It was none other than Bob Fletcher, the dog shelter manager who had been arrested recently for his treatment of the dogs there. Winston looked up at him, and as he did, Bob noticed him from outside and pointed threateningly at the poor little Pug.

Winston began to bark angrily and growled and grunted. He didn't like Bob and sensed that he was up to no good. As Bob fiddled with the lock on the patio doors to try to gain entry, Winston jumped up and down, barking incessantly. He bared his teeth and tried to be as aggressive as he could with Bob. But Bob was undeterred and continued to fiddle with the lock.

Out of desperation, Winston ran through to the front of the house and ran up to the front door. He pawed at the front door, as if he was trying to open it. And then he began to howl as loud as he could. He howled again and again as if he was in severe pain. He got louder and louder as he became more worried about what Bob was up to.

Bob could hear the howling and it made him even more desperate to get inside the cottage before someone heard. He struggled to pick the lock as his hands began to shake. But after a few more moments of frustration, he finally unlocked the patio doors and walked into the cottage. Shutting the door behind him, he could still hear the howling coming from the front of the house. He squinted his eyes which made him look very evil. And he rolled his sleeves up. He wanted revenge for what Alison had done. He strode forward with purpose to confront poor little Winston.

At the same time, Alison and Becky reached the summit of the hill and looked out across the valley beneath them. It was completely covered in snow. They could see a church in the distance, and a small hamlet. They also saw fields and fields of the whitest and purest snow.

'We made it to the top. Well done Becky', said Alison.

'It's a beautiful view. And the sky is so blue. There isn't a cloud in the sky', said Becky. The sun shone down on them and they stood there for a while to catch their breaths back. 'I hope Winston is okay?'

Alison smiled and gave Becky a big hug. 'I am sure he's fine. He's probably asleep right now. We will probably wake him up when we return'. Becky reciprocated her mother's smile and looked out again at the beautiful landscape.

'I wish he could talk. Wouldn't that be funny?'

'Very funny. He would be a wonder dog!' said Alison. She then put her arm round Becky as they surveyed the winter scene around them.

Bob Fletcher walked straight through the kitchen and into the hallway where he confronted the little Pug. Winston was still howling and barking, and scraping at the front door. When he felt someone was behind him, he turned around and saw Bob staring at him with evil intent in his eyes. Winston then continued to howl as loud as he could.

'There's no one here to help you, Winston. You are out of luck. They've gone out. And I'm here to take revenge on your idiotic owner. She shopped me to the Police; and she needs to be taught a lesson. Unfortunately, you are causing too much noise. I'm gonna have to shut you up once and for all, aren't I?'

As if he understood what Bob had said, Winston suddenly howled as loud as he could. It was so loud that Bob was deafened for a moment.

'Come here! You little brat! It's about time you were taught a lesson in manners!' said Bob, who stepped forward and crouched down to try and pick Winston up. Winston growled and bared his teeth angrily. It was a valiant effort from Winston, but the odds were highly stacked against him. As Winston continued to growl, he could see what looked like a baseball bat that was by Bob's side. Bob must have brought it in with him. He was probably intending to wreck the place, not before he had taken care of poor little Winston.

Just then, Peter the Postman was walking by. He wasn't delivering at Alison's house today, but he was on his usual post round. He heard the howling and the barking, and thought that it sounded very strange. Only a few days ago, he had met the little Pug and had thought he seemed so gentle and kind natured. He also wondered why the dog was so distressed. Call it intuition, but he stopped what he was doing and walked up to the front door. He could hear the dog was just on the other side of the door. He opened the letterbox and peered inside. He couldn't see the dog but he guessed it was directly below. But he did see Bob Fletcher wielding a baseball bat and looking very angry.

'What are you up to, Bob? Stop what you are doing right now!' shouted Peter. Bob got a shock and for a few seconds, he froze with bat in hand. As he did, Winston quickly ran through Bob's legs and out through the kitchen and into the laundry room. He reached the back patio doors, only to find them shut. He scraped at the back door in the hope of somehow opening it. As he did, Peter appeared around the back. Winston jumped out of the way to let Peter in. As Peter walked through into the kitchen, Winston jumped behind a plant pot out of sight.

'Stay back! Stay back!' shouted Bob to Peter when they met in the hallway. 'I've got nothing to lose! I'll use this on you if I have to'. He continued to wield the baseball bat.

'Bob, don't make things worse. You have got lots to lose. If you assault me, you will spend years in jail. Is that what you want? To be in prison for years. And to have my death on your conscience. Put the bat down, Bob. You are way better than that', said Peter calmly.

Bob remained motionless with the baseball bat in both hands, as if ready to hit an oncoming ball.

'It's Christmas, Bob. Do you want to spend Christmas in jail? Your wife will divorce you, your kids will disown you. Don't be silly. You still have a lot going for you. Put the bat down. Please.....' said Peter. Bob didn't know what to do. He looked at Peter, and then looked at the bat. His gaze then dropped to the floor. He relaxed his grip on the bat and lowered it and then dropped it onto the hallway floor.

'That's good, Bob. You've done the right thing. Now, I want you to walk through to the laundry room. There is a seat in there. I want you to sit on it and let me call the Police', said Peter. Bob looked at Peter suddenly with fear in his eyes. And for a split second, Peter thought Bob was going to pick up the bat and resume where they left off. But Bob's gaze again dropped to the floor as if he was resigned to his fate. 'It's better this way. If you try to escape, it will look worse for you', continued Peter.

They both walked into the laundry room and Bob sat down on the wooden chair in there. As he did, he could see two eyes peering out from above the plant pot in the corner. Winston looked at him with fear in his eyes. But Bob just looked away, dejected. As he sat there, he began to cry silently. Peter noticed this and put his hand on Bob's shoulder.

'Bob, you need to get some help. I will speak to the Police when they arrive'. And Peter went outside the double patio doors and walked around the back garden to make a phone call to the Police. Again, Winston peered over the plant pot and looked at his old master, now weeping with his head in his hands. Winston remained silent and didn't take his eyes off Bob.

About 25 minutes later, Becky and Alison were walking back down the hill and reached the bottom of the track. They could see the road ahead which meandered down to their cottage.

'I really enjoyed our walk', said Becky. 'I love the fresh air. And I love the snow. It's magical. And so Christmassy. I can't believe it's only 3 days till Christmas. I can't believe it'.

Alison smiled at her. 'Yes, Christmas is upon us. And you already have your main present. Santa knows all about it; he knows that you got Winston. So don't expect loads of presents off him'.

'I won't, Mom. I don't need any more presents. Winston is all I want', said Becky with a gleaming smile on her face.

As they walked down the side of the road, they caught sight of their little cottage up ahead. Alison thought she could see a vehicle outside and squinted her eyes. The winter sun was shining down on the snow and nearly blinding her as she walked along the road. A slight worry set in, and she wanted to know if she was right. She started to walk a bit quicker.

'Mom, what's wrong?' said Becky.

'I don't know. But let's walk a little quicker. Come on'.

As they got within 100 metres of their cottage, they could clearly see a police car on the road outside their house. Alison feared what may have happened and covered her mouth with her hand in shock.

'Mom, why is there a police car outside our house?' asked Becky.

'I don't know, but I intend to find out', replied Alison.

They walked ever quicker until they reached the driveway to their cottage. Just then, Bob Fletcher was being escorted off the premises by a police officer. Alison stood back and kept Becky behind her as Bob walked to the back of the police car. He was in handcuffs. He looked at Alison momentarily but said nothing. The police officer motioned for him to get in the back of the car, which he did, and then the officer shut the car door behind him.

From the entrance to the driveway, Peter said, 'Officer! I can tell Alison what happened, if you like'.

'Thanks, sir', said the officer who then got into the police car and drove off.

Alison and Becky ran down to speak to Peter. 'What's happened, Peter?' asked Alison. 'Is Winston okay?' shouted Becky.

'Everything is okay. Winston is fine. He is in the laundry room', replied Peter. He then explained what had happened. As he continued to speak, tears of shock and relief welled up in Alison's eyes. And Peter put his arm around her to comfort her. Meanwhile, Becky had run into the back garden and opened the patio doors. She looked all around the laundry room and couldn't see hide nor hair of

Winston. She ran through to the kitchen and then into the hallway.

'Winston!' she shouted as she saw him hiding under his blanket. 'We're back and you are safe! It's all over. You are safe!' His eyes peeked from underneath the blanket and looked sorrowfully at her. He slowly got up and shook the blanket off him and trotted over to her. She held her hands out to him and he ran into them, embracing her. She gave him the biggest cuddle ever and kissed him again and again.

'It's all over. You are safe', she said, and began to cry profusely. Fighting back the tears, she said, 'I won't leave you ever again. I love you Winston'. She began to cradle him in her arms and she felt the warmth of his body against hers. She gently stroked his back. He calmed down and began to breathe more normally. He now felt safe, in Becky's arms. He had been through an ordeal. But it was now all over.

Alison walked into the hallway and saw the two of them together. 'Becky, do you realise what happened? Winston saved the day! If it wasn't for him barking and howling, Peter wouldn't have checked on the house. He didn't like what he heard, so he took a look. Winston got Bob caught. How amazing is that?'

Becky raised Winston up so that his feet were dangling down below him and his face was level with hers. 'You are a super dog! I knew it! You saved the day Winston! Yay!' And she lay him against her shoulder and gave him another cuddle. Alison, who was standing nearby, smiled and then walked over to Becky and Winston and gave him a pat on the head.

CHRISTMAS DAY

It was beautiful outside. The snow had been falling overnight and when little Winston woke up in Becky's bed and looked out of the window, he could see snowflakes coming down from the sky and another blanket of snow on the garden. He loved the sight of snow, but so far hadn't been allowed to play in it. He didn't know why. He fixed his eyes on the tree outside and could see a couple of Robins playing together. He wished he could go outside and play in the snow.

He looked at his new best friend, Becky, who was asleep. She looked so happy and serene in bed. He sniffed her face and then gave her cheek a lick, which woke her up. When she opened her eyes, she was looking straight at Winston's face.

'Oh Winston, aren't you a cutie?' she said. 'Good morning. Merry Christmas Winston!' She pulled him closer to her and gave him a hug. He licked her face again and they lay side by side for a while. Both of them were still half asleep, but both looked very happy. A few minutes later, Becky opened her eyes again. It was Christmas Day. She should get up. No doubt Santa had been and had left some presents under the Christmas tree.

'Come on Winston. Santa was here last night. And I know that there are a couple of presents under the tree for you. So let's go find out', said Becky to Winston.

They both got up off the bed. Winston jumped down on the floor and stretched his legs and yawned. Becky jumped out of bed and put on her dressing gown over her pyjamas. They both walked into the sitting room, and Becky opened the curtains to let in the daylight. She then turned on the Christmas tree lights and Winston looked at them in wonder.

'Oh, Winston, I can see presents under the tree. But I already know that you are my main Christmas present, and I couldn't have wished for anything more', she said, as she hugged him again.

'I thought I would find you both in here', said her mother, who was standing in her dressing gown in the doorway. 'Merry Christmas Becky and Winston!' Alison went over to Becky and gave her a kiss and a cuddle, and then she cuddled little Winston.

'Mom, where are Winston's presents? Are they here?' said Becky.

'Yes, those two are his', replied Alison.

Becky gave them to Winston, who first began to sniff them and then after a few moments, he tore the Christmas wrapping paper to shreds, and eventually found his presents inside.

'Look what you got for Christmas, Winston!' said Becky. 'It's a Christmas jumper and a Christmas coat. So you can keep warm, and we can take you outside if you wear your coat. Isn't that nice Winston?'

He looked at her and stared intently into her eyes.

'Let's put your jumper on', she said. And after a minute or two, she had negotiated him into his Christmas jumper. 'That will keep you warm, won't it?'

Alison smiled when she saw Winston with his new jumper on. She got down on her knees and held Winston's paws in her hands, and said, 'Winston, do you realise that you saved Christmas for all those dogs in the shelter? If I hadn't fallen in love with you when I saw your picture on their website, I would never have gone to the shelter. And now that they have closed it down and the dogs have been housed elsewhere by the ASPCA, you saved Christmas for them! Some may still be looking for a permanent new home, but at least they didn't spend Christmas with that evil man, Bob Fletcher'.

'It's all thanks to you, Winston', said Becky, and she gave him the biggest hug ever.

THE END

ABOUT THE AUTHOR

Jenn Somerville loves writing about families, friendship, dogs and romance. Her short stories and novellas are available on Amazon and in Kindle Unlimited.

A self-confessed television addict, dog lover, and hopeless romantic, Jenn loves nothing more than the thrill of sharing her stories with others.

SPECIAL THANKS

I would like to thank you for reading!

I really hope that you enjoyed this story and I look forward to hearing any feedback you have on it by way of review (on Amazon and Goodreads websites).

JOIN MY MAILING LIST

Never miss the next book in the series

Never miss a limited time offer

Never miss a free story or freebie!

Join my mailing list by going to https://fantastic-builder-2533.ck.page/b554c54593